SLEEPING BEAUTY

FOR JOEL AND JOHN

This edition first published in the United Kingdom in 2016 by
Pavilion Children's Books
1 Gower Street
London
WC1E 6HD

An imprint of Pavilion Books Company Limited

A CIP catalogue record for this book is available from the British Library.

ISBN: 9781843652915

Reproduction by Tag Publishing, UK
Printed and bound by 1010 Printing International Ltd, China
10 9 8 7 6 5 4 3 2 1

This book can be ordered direct from the publisher at the website:
www.pavilionbooks.com, or try your local bookshop.

SLEEPING BEAUTY

A mid-century fairy tale

David Roberts

Retold by
Lynn Roberts-Maloney

PAVILION

In a time not too long ago and in a land much like our own, there was a happy young girl called Annabel. She lived with her two aunts, Rosalind and Flora. Annabel loved science fiction and spent hours dreaming of the future, unaware that she was living under an evil spell that could mean she had no future at all.

On Annabel's first birthday something had happened to change her future forever. All the neighbours were invited to a party, but one of them was a mean and spiteful witch called Morwenna. She was jealous of Rosalind, Flora and the beautiful baby Annabel, so she set out to spoil the fun.

All the guests fussed over baby Annabel and gave her gifts. They were having a wonderful time until Morwenna stepped forward.

"Here's *my* gift" she cried, casting a spell. "Before her 16th birthday is over, she will prick her finger on a needle and die!" In a flash Morwenna disappeared, leaving behind only the echo of an evil laugh.

Rosalind cried in despair, afraid that she could do nothing to stop the spell from coming true. But Flora, who was a good and kind witch, said "Morwenna is powerful and her spell is strong. I can't take the spell away… but I can change it. If Annabel pricks her finger she will not die, but will sleep for a thousand years."

To avoid upsetting Rosalind further, Flora kept a secret. Morwenna's spell was so strong that if Annabel was not woken at exactly midnight on the last day of the thousand years she would indeed die.

Rosalind removed every needle from their home and kept a careful watch over Annabel. Oblivious to her fate, Annabel spent her time reading space books and watching television. She marvelled at the films and stories about science and robots. She often thought that if she could wish for anything, it would be to see the world as it is in the future.

Annabel's 16th birthday arrived. Rosalind was so relieved that Annabel would be 16 and the spell would be lifted that she let her guard down and did not notice that a large present wrapped in shiny paper had been delivered to the house.

Annabel excitedly tore off the paper. Inside was a record player. This was something Annabel had desperately wanted but had not been allowed to have. "It must be a surprise gift from my aunts," she thought happily.

But it wasn't from her aunts. Morwenna had left the gift, and she spied

through the window as Annabel put the record on. In her excitement Annabel

pricked her finger on the needle. In an instant she fell to the floor asleep.

The spell had come true.

When Rosalind found Annabel she was inconsolable. "How will I protect her? I cannot watch over her for 1000 years," she sobbed. Flora had an idea.

"Rosalind become a rose
Do not shed any tears
Grow with magic, grow with love
Guard Annabel for a thousand years."

In a shimmer of golden light Rosalind began to change. She became a rose tree, which grew and grew. Out of the windows and doors thick vines and thorns entwined to leave no sign of what lay beneath. Flora wrote down the story so that it would never be forgotten. She called it *Sleeping Beauty*. She then turned herself into a light, so Annabel was not in darkness.

Many, many years went by and the world saw many changes

but the rose tree remained.

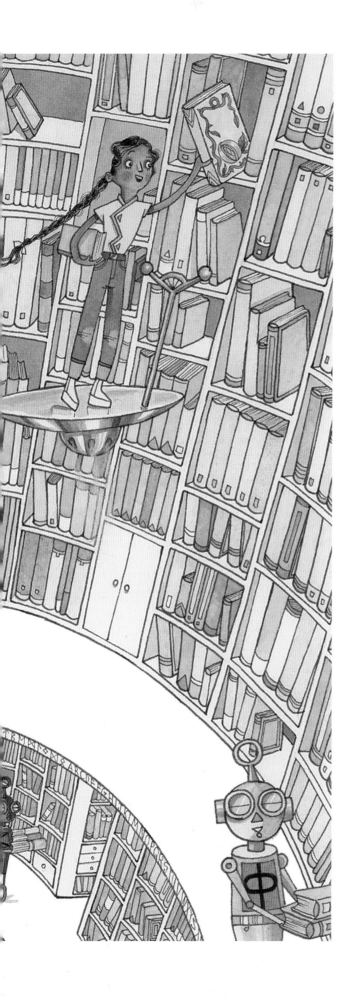

A thousand years passed and a young girl called Zoe was researching the history of the giant rose tree. She wondered why it still stood when everything around it had changed so much. She set off to the library to find out more.

In the library Zoe found a collection of very old and dusty books. She loved books and history and finding out about what life used to be like. She often thought that if she could wish for anything, it would be to see the world as it was in the past.

Zoe found a book with a rose on the cover. It was called *Sleeping Beauty*.
As she looked through the pages, she became convinced that the story was true.

When she saw that it was exactly 1000 years to the day since it was written she
took the book and ran from the library.

Off she rushed to the rose tree as fast as she could. She had just a few hours
until midnight to help Sleeping Beauty.

At the rose tree, Zoe fought her way
through the vines, crawling over giant
thorns and brushing aside enormous
petals. Time ticked by and in the
gloom Zoe was lost. Suddenly
in the distance she saw a light. It was
Flora's light and it led Zoe to the house
hidden deep within the great rose.

Opening the door she was amazed at what she saw. "It's like a museum," she said, going into each room. On opening the last door, she saw the girl, asleep. "Sleeping Beauty," she whispered. As the clock began to strike midnight she reached out and touched the sleeping girl's hand.

As their fingers met, Annabel's eyes opened. "I feel like I've been asleep for ages," she said "I hope I haven't missed my 16th birthday."

Zoe stared at her "No, you haven't missed your birthday, but you are not 16. You are 1016! You are the youngest-looking oldest person ever!" she exclaimed.

Zoe sat down beside Annabel. She showed her the book and told her the whole tale. Annabel laughed and cried as she realised her life, as she knew it, was gone. She looked at the shining light and the rose tree that had once surrounded her house as it slowly receded to one small bud.

"Thank you my dear Aunts," she whispered,

"You've kept me safe for 1000 years."

Annabel's sadness turned to excitement and she ran to the door, desperate to see what the world was like. "Come on," she said, taking Zoe's hand "Show me the future," and they stepped out together into the bright morning sunshine.

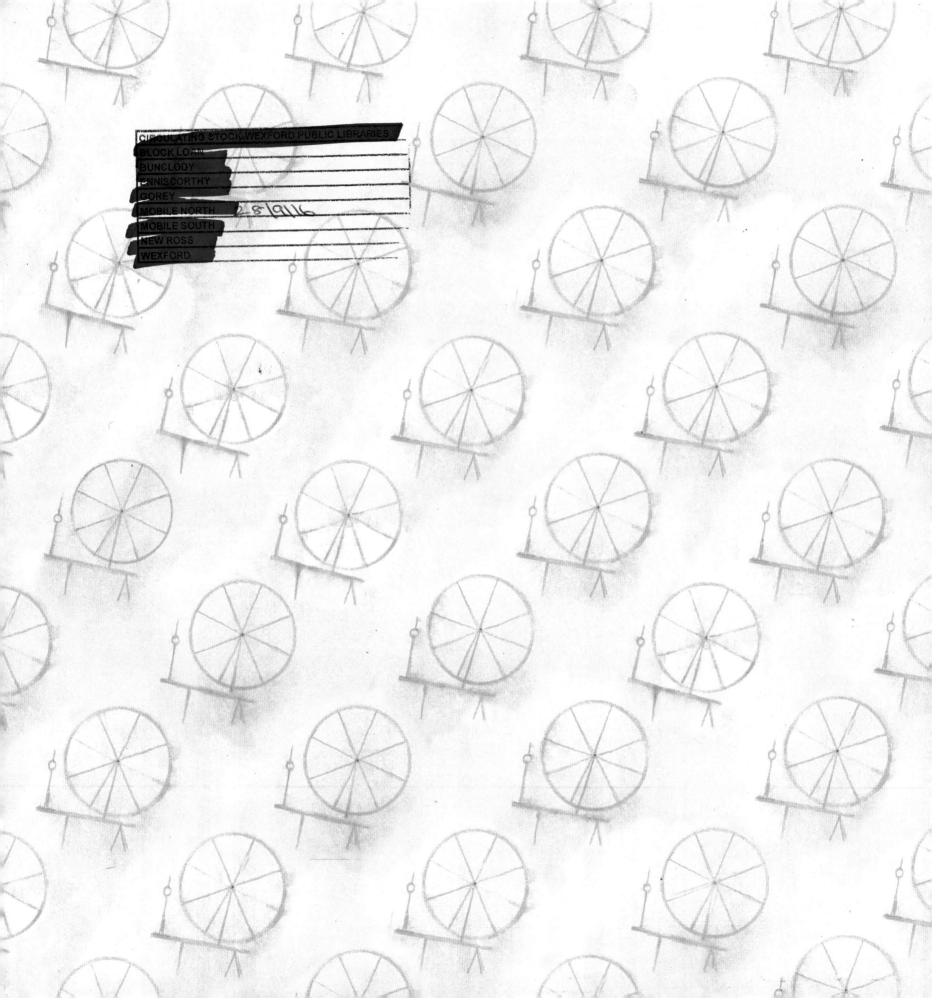